This book belongs to

....

....

CONTENTS

Illustrations by Stuart Trotter
Stories by Stuart Trotter
Text and couplets by Cathy Jones
Activities by Jenny Bak
Designed by Martin Aggett

THE
RUPERT
ANNUAL

EXPRESS NEWSPAPERS

EGMONT
We bring stories to life

Published in Great Britain 2009 by Egmont UK Limited
239 Kensington High Street, London W8 6SA
Rupert Bear™: © 2009 Classic Media Distribution Limited/Express Newspapers.
All Rights Reserved.

ISBN 978 1 4052 4401 5
Printed in Italy

No. 74

£7.99

MAP OF NUTWOOD

Welcome to Nutwood, home to Rupert and his friends for 90 years! This charming world and its inhabitants were created by Mary Tourtel, who produced the first Rupert comic for the *Daily Express* on 8 November 1920. Since then, other writers and artists have taken up her work, establishing Rupert as a classic character beloved by generations of children.

RUPERT

and the

Dam

RUPERT HEARS THE TREE SNAP

When Rupert looks out to the yard,
He sees the wind is blowing hard.

Says Mum: "Oh, what a stormy day!"
As all her washing flies away.

Young Rupert brings the washing back,
Then, suddenly, he hears a CRACK!

And with dismay, Dad goes to see.
The wind has snapped the apple tree.

"What a stormy day," Rupert thinks as he looks out the window. Outside in the yard, Mrs Bear is struggling with the washing line. Rupert goes to lend a hand.

"Would you like some help?" he asks.

"Yes, please, Rupert," she says. "I've never known such windy weather."

Every time Mrs Bear reaches up to grasp the washing, it flaps away from her. Mrs Bear and Rupert laugh as she tries to catch the sheets.

Rupert's dad is in the garden too. Mr Bear is worried about a young apple tree that's bending over as the wind whips around it, swirling this way and that. Rupert goes to see when suddenly, *CRACK*, the trunk snaps in half!

"Oh dear me," says Mr Bear. He is very upset.

"Will it grow back again?" asks Rupert.

"I don't think we'll be able to save it," says Mr Bear. "The trunk has snapped too low down."

RUPERT RUNS TO SEE THE FLOOD

Bill Badger comes to tell his friend
The stream is flooding at the bend.

The two friends run to take a look
Into the swollen, rushing brook.

The water swirls below the pair.
The river bank's no longer there!

Just then, old Gaffer comes along.
"Is something fishy going on?"

Rupert is still thinking about the tree when he hears someone calling his name. He looks up to see Bill Badger. He's come to tell Rupert some exciting news.

"I've just been down by the stream," shouts Bill over the howling wind. "It's flooding – come and see!"

Rupert tells his dad where they are going.

"Be careful near the water, you two," warns Mr Bear. "The current will be stronger than usual while the stream is in flood."

"We will!" Rupert and Bill follow the rushing brook down to the river. Here, the water is lapping over the bank and the path alongside the river has disappeared completely under the water.

The two friends spot old Gaffer leaning on his stick, gazing at the river.

" It's been many a long year since I've seen the river water this high," says old Gaffer. "Something fishy is going on, you mark my words."

Rupert and the Dam

RUPERT FINDS A STICK

The two chums gaze into the stream.
Shapes underwater dart and gleam.

And then, one little fish breaks rank.
It flicks a stick on to the bank!

The stick is long and very straight.
It's carved with patterns, quite ornate.

"I wonder what this stick could be?
Old Sailor Sam might know. Let's see."

Rupert and Bill wonder what old Gaffer can mean. Gingerly, they make their way closer to the water's edge and stoop to look into the swirling water. Down in the depths, they see dark shapes darting about.

Suddenly, something leaps right out of the water. Rupert and Bill jump back in alarm.

It's a golden fish. The fish flicks a small stick up onto the riverbank, and then splashes back into the river.

"Wait!" calls Rupert, but the fish is gone.

Rupert picks up the stick and the two friends examine it. It has carved patterns all over.

"Do you think it belongs to someone?" asks Bill.

"I think it must," says Rupert. "We should try to return it to its owner."

"But how can we find out who it belongs to?" asks Bill, scratching his head.

"Well, it came from the water," says Rupert, "so perhaps Sailor Sam might know."

But Sailor Sam is puzzled, too.
"I'm not sure what it's meant to do.

"But it's a magic wand, I fear,
So we should get it out of here.

"While all this water is about,
I'll try my new invention out."

In Sam's amphibious car they go,
And head upstream against the flow.

The friends tell Sailor Sam about the flood and the fish, and they show him the mysterious stick.

"Hmm," says Sailor Sam, "I've never seen the like before. The patterns are so delicate."

"They look like tiny tooth marks," says Rupert.

"I think it looks like a magic wand," ventures Bill.

Then Sailor Sam has an idea. He takes the friends to see his new invention.

It's a *very* strange-looking car!

"This is an amphibious vehicle," says Sailor Sam proudly. "It can travel on land and in the water."

Rupert and Bill are agog.

"While all this water is about, I think I'll try it out. Let's see if we can discover where this weird object came from. Hop aboard!"

So they all scramble in the car and Sailor Sam sets sail. Soon the water is lapping around the tyres as the amphibious car heads upstream against the current.

RUPERT RIDES IN THE AMPHIBIOUS CAR

Then Rupert gives a sudden shout,
Dark shapes beneath them swim about.

"Look, there!" cries Rupert. "It would seem
That something's followed us upstream."

Then Sailor Sam says with dismay,
"We're stuck! A dam is in our way."

The dam is made of wood and rushes,
But through a gap the water gushes.

The floodwater rushes past the car, swirling around the trees and lapping over the bank. Rupert and Bill timidly peer over the side. Dark shapes flit and glide below them.

"I can see things in the water," Rupert calls over the sound of the engine, "but they seem too big to be fish."

"What else could they be?" shouts Bill, and then the unknown creatures suddenly overtake them and appear ahead of the amphibious car.

The friends are so busy watching the mysterious shapes in the water that they don't notice an obstruction up ahead.

"Hold on tight!" shouts Sailor Sam, and he throws the engine into reverse to slow the car. They drift to a stop beneath a huge dam built of wooden logs and rushes woven neatly together. In the middle, there's a big gap where some of the logs have broken and water is gushing through.

RUPERT MEETS THE BEAVER SCOUT

Just then, a furry head pops out.
"Hello! I am the beaver scout.

"Our lodge was damaged by the rains.
We need that stick back," he explains.

"Please follow me. Now, come this way."
The scout turns tail and swims away.

Sailor Sam pulls on a lever –
Down they dive, after the beaver.

Then Rupert sees two of the dark shapes growing bigger and bigger until, suddenly, two furry heads pop out of the water.

"Hello! I'm the beaver scout," says the first beaver. "This dam is part of our beaver lodge, but part of it washed away in the storm."

"Can we do anything to help?" asks Rupert.

"We need that stick most urgently," says the second beaver. "Follow us."

And they dive back under the water.

"Oh dear!" says Bill. "We can't follow the beavers down there. Whatever shall we do?"

But Sailor Sam has another surprise for the two friends. He presses a switch on the control panel and a glass roof slides silently across. Then he pulls some levers and the vehicle tips its nose down into the water and dives after the two beavers. Rupert and Bill look at each other in amazement.

RUPERT ENTERS THE BEAVER LODGE

And then, beneath the lodge they wait
To enter through a secret gate.

It's opened by the beaver scout.
The chums gaze round as they climb out.

The beaver scout, without delay,
Leads them along a passageway.

They stand before a massive door.
The scout knocks hard. They wait once more.

Soon they arrive at a secret gate, hidden behind some waterweed.

The beaver scout opens the gate and they drive inside. They go a little further before the car comes to a stop next to some dry land.

Sailor Sam pushes a button and the glass roof slides open. The chums step out and gaze around at giant reeds while Sailor Sam ties the amphibious car to its mooring.

"Follow me," says the beaver scout urgently.

He leads Sailor Sam, Rupert and Bill along a winding passageway lined on either side with tall rushes. They pass many mysterious doors along the way, but they have to hurry on to keep up with the beaver scout. Finally, they arrive at a massive wooden door. The beaver scout stops, stands up straight and knocks firmly three times. The sound of the knocks echoes down the corridor.

RUPERT MEETS THE BEAVER KING

"Enter!" a deep, gruff voice replies.
And then the friends get a surprise!

They stand before the Beaver King.
And Rupert squeaks, "We found something."

The king growls back, "Is this a trick?"
So Rupert shows the king his stick.

"I thought my wand was lost forever
When it fell into the river!"

"Enter!" a gruff voice booms from the other side of the door.

The beaver scout beckons to the friends and pushes on the heavy door. It swings slowly back and Rupert, Bill and Sailor Sam enter a huge reedy hall. They gasp with surprise to see a giant beaver awaiting them.

The scout approaches the Beaver King and whispers urgently into his ear. When he has finished, the Beaver King glares angrily at the three friends.

"We've found something that might belong to you," says Rupert. "It's a carved stick."

"What? Is this a trick?" the Beaver King roars.

But Rupert holds up the stick and the Beaver King gasps. He takes the stick from Rupert and looks at it carefully. He runs his paw over the carved patterns.

"It's my wand!" he cries. "I thought this had been lost forever when the storm broke the dam and it was washed away in the flood."

RUPERT FOLLOWS THE BEAVER KING

The king smiles, "This is very good –
Without this wand we have no wood.

"But we can build a new lodge now.
So follow me, I'll show you how."

He tells them how they chew and gnaw
Trees growing on the woodland floor.

They cross the dam in single file.
The leak is gushing all the while.

The Beaver King smiles.

"This is very good," he says to Rupert. "This wand is very important to us beavers. You see, without it, we would have no wood. And without wood, we cannot mend the dam or repair our lodge."

"How does the wand help you to get the wood you need?" asks Rupert, puzzled.

"Follow me, and I will show you," says the Beaver King.

It's tricky keeping up with the Beaver King. The friends clamber over reeds and scramble through rushes until they arrive in a quiet woodland clearing.

"This is where we grow our wood," says the Beaver King.

"How do you chop it down?" asks Rupert.

"Our special teeth are strong enough to gnaw the wood," explains the Beaver King. "We eat the tree bark and use the wood inside for building."

*The friends emerge now from the shade
Into a quiet woodland glade.*

*"After my wand was washed away,
The wood ran out within a day!*

*"Now I can re-grow all the trees,
To cut new wood will be a breeze.*

*"We'll mend the lodge with sticks and mud,
And soon the dam will stop the flood."*

"We cut the wood into logs and then we carry them to the river where we built the dam. The lodge where we live is a part of the dam, so it is very important to repair it when it gets damaged." The Beaver King sighs. "When the wand was lost we quickly ran out of wood."

"But I still don't understand. How does the wand help you?" asks Rupert.

"I'll show you," says the Beaver King.

He holds the wand and taps lightly on a tree stump. In a flash of magic, the tree instantly re-grows before their very eyes. Rupert and Bill are amazed.

"Well, I've never seen the like!" exclaims Sailor Sam, rubbing his eyes in disbelief.

"Now we'll have all the wood we need to mend the hole in the dam!" laughs the Beaver King.

And, without delay, the clever beavers begin to make their repairs.

RUPERT'S WAND DOES MAGIC!

The King smiles, "This new wand's for you.
You'll see what magic it can do."

They wave goodbye. The new friends beam,
As Sailor Sam sets off downstream.

Back home, young Rupert tells his dad
Of the excitement he has had.

When Rupert taps the trunk … one, two …
The apple tree's as good as new!

"When the dam has been repaired, the flood will stop," says the Beaver King, "so you have helped save the beavers and Nutwood!"

The Beaver King presents Rupert with a small stick. It looks just like the wand, and it's covered with the same curious carvings. "This is for you," he says. "Just see what magic it can do!"

Rupert is very pleased and thanks the Beaver King as they make their way back to Sam's amphibious car.

Mr and Mrs Bear are in the garden when Rupert hurries down the path. He tells them all about his adventure and how he met the Beaver King.

"Just look what he gave me," says Rupert excitedly, showing them the magic wand.

"Well, well," says Rupert's dad. "I wonder if it will work on our poor little apple tree."

So Rupert taps the trunk gently and, in a flash of magic, the apple tree's restored as good as new!

SECRET DECODER

What kind of tree grows two by two?

A B C D E F G H I J K L M

_ _ _ _ _ _ _ _ _ _ _ _ _

N O P Q R S T U V W X Y Z

_ _ _ _ _ _ _ _ _ _ _ _ _

The answer is:

_ _ _ _ _ _ _ _ _
Z   K V Z I   G I V V

The Beaver King has given Rupert a puzzle to solve.
Use the decoder to reveal the answer!

The decoder: Underneath each letter above, write the letters of the alphabet backwards, starting with Z under A, Y under B, and so on. Decode each letter of the answer and write them in the blank spaces to solve the riddle!

RUPERT'S COLOURING

Colour in the big picture using the image on the left as a reference. You could be really creative and use different colours too!

"What an exciting ride!" says Bill Badger, as he and Rupert climb out of Sailor Sam's amphibious car.

RUPERT
and the
Golden Carp

RUPERT FINDS AN OLD KITE

"It's such a very windy day,"
Thinks Rupert Bear, "what shall I play?"

But here comes Algy Pug to say,
"Let's go and fly our kites today."

So Rupert searches on his shelf,
"Look! Here's a kite I made myself."

And off to Nutwood's park they run
To join in all the outdoor fun.

It's a very windy morning and Rupert is wondering what to do. As he looks out of the window, he sees Algy Pug coming up the garden path with something tucked under his arm. Rupert hurries to the door and opens it before Algy has a chance to knock.

"Hello," says Rupert. "What have you got there?"

"It's my kite," replies Algy. "Everyone is flying kites on the Common. Are you coming?"

"Yes!" exclaims Rupert. "I'll fetch my old kite."

The pals go to Rupert's room where they hunt around for his kite. They find it lying on a high shelf.

"Here it is," says Rupert, blowing off the dust. "I made this old kite ages ago. It's a bit battered now, but I think it will still fly."

The two friends set off for Nutwood Common with their kites. As they make their way past the trees towards open ground, they spot a crowd of kite-fliers and hurry towards them.

RUPERT'S STRING BREAKS

All Rupert's chums have gathered there,
To fly their kites high in the air.

"Some of these kites are very smart –
Just look at how they swoop and dart!"

But Rupert's old kite still flies well.
That it's homemade, you could not tell.

Then, as the wind tugs at his kite,
The string snaps and the kite takes flight!

Edward Trunk and Bill Badger are already flying their kites. Rupert and Algy stop to watch them. Their kites soar high into the air, then swoop and dive. Then Edward and Bill spot their friends watching and run over to meet them.

"Hello," says Edward. "Come and join in the fun!"

"The weather is perfect for kite-flying," adds Bill.

"Your kites look very smart," says Rupert looking dubiously at his old homemade kite. "I'm not sure if my old kite is strong enough for this wind."

But Rupert and Algy join the others, trailing their kites behind them. Rupert's kite catches an updraught and the wind carries it soaring high into the sky. Rupert is very pleased that his old homemade kite is flying so well, but a sudden gust tugs at the kite string. The old string is not strong enough and it snaps!

Rupert is left holding a dangling string as he watches his kite being whisked away over the Common.

RUPERT SEES AN AIRSHIP

It's whipped off on a gusty breeze,
Across the Common, toward the trees.

Poor Rupert runs after his kite,
But in the woods he loses sight.

Then Edward points up in a tree,
"What is that orange shape I see?"

A weird craft hovers in the air.
Says Rupert: "What's that doing there?"

"Oh, no!" cries Rupert. "My kite is flying away."
Edward Trunk is standing near Rupert and hears
him shout. "Let's chase after it!" he says.

The pair race across Nutwood Common towards the
wood, but the kite is travelling very fast and soon it's
just a speck in the distance. It hovers above the trees
and then dips out of view. By the time Rupert and
Edward reach the wood, the kite is nowhere to be seen.

Rupert searches along the path and through the
wood, but he has no luck – there's no sign of his kite
anywhere. Then he hears a shout. Edward has found
something.

Rupert joins him beneath a tall beech tree. Edward
points up through the branches. Rupert peers towards
the sky, but it isn't his kite Edward has spotted.
A strangely-shaped object hovers above them.

"It's some sort of airship," Rupert murmurs.
"I wonder what it's doing here?"

*He clambers down, and from his perch
He spies a friend to join the search.*

*"The Chinese Conjurer just might
Help me to find my missing kite!"*

*The Conjurer and his strange guest
Agree to Rupert's grave request.*

*The two men help him find his kite,
But it's a pretty sorry sight!*

Edward helps Rupert clamber up into the tree.
"Can you see your kite?" calls Edward from the bottom of the tree.
"No," Rupert calls back, "but I can see someone who might help us search for it." Rupert has spotted the Chinese Conjurer, with another gentleman who is a stranger to Nutwood. "Let's ask them if they'll help us," he says.
The chums hurry over to the two men.

"I'm sorry to bother you," interrupts Rupert, "but I've lost my kite. I wonder if you've seen it anywhere?"
The Conjurer speaks to his guest in Chinese and then turns back to Rupert. "We believe we can help with your request," he smiles.
The two gentlemen walk off into the undergrowth and very soon hold up Rupert's kite.
"Hurray!" cries Rupert, but he soon realises that the kite came down in a bramble bush and now it's torn.

Rupert and the Golden Carp

RUPERT LEARNS OF THE KITE FESTIVAL

The Conjurer now tells the pair
About a grand kite-flying fair.

"I cannot go along this year,
But I've a plan that you must hear.

"So, come back to my home, you two,
And I'll explain what you can do.

"Now, you and Tigerlily might
Go in my place, and fly my kite."

"Thank you for helping me find my kite," says Rupert politely, but the Chinese Conjurer can see that Rupert is disappointed.

"I'm sorry about your kite," the Chinese Conjurer says, "but you two might be just the pair to help me. An annual kite-flying festival is about to begin, and I always make a very special kite to fly in honour of the Emperor. Unfortunately, this year I am unable to attend in person."

Rupert and Edward follow the Chinese Conjurer and his guest back to the Pagoda. As they approach they see the Conjurer's daughter, Tigerlily, waiting for them. She smiles and waves.

"I believe these two friends of yours may solve our problem," the Chinese Conjurer greets her.

"What can we do to help?" Rupert enquires.

"If you accompany Tigerlily to the festival," explains the Conjurer, "then you can fly the kite in my place!"

RUPERT IS GIVEN A SPECIAL KITE

He shows the friends a yellow sack.
He takes it out, and then turns back.

"If you will do this thing for me,
Then I will fix your kite, you'll see!

"This bag contains a magic kite,
So please don't let it out of sight.

"You must not open it at all
Until you're at the festival."

"It would certainly be a great honour!" exclaims Rupert excitedly. But then he looks glumly at his broken kite.

"Don't worry about that," says Tigerlily kindly. "My father will fix it for you, you'll see."

The Chinese Conjurer unlocks a glass cabinet, and takes out a yellow silk bag. Gently, he hands the bag to Rupert, who takes it with both hands. Ruper is amazed to discover that it's as light as a feather!

"This bag contains a special kite," continues the Chinese Conjurer solemnly, "which has magical properties. You must not let it out of the bag until you are at the festival."

"How will we get to the kite festival?" asks Rupert.

"The Emperor has sent an airship to take you there," the Chinese Conjurer smiles. "The Emperor will be there to greet you, but before you go, you must both get your parents' permission."

Excitedly, the two good chums
Set off for home to tell their mums.

At Rupert's house he has to ask
His mum if he can do the task.

"Enjoy the trip," says Mrs Bear.
"Have lots of fun, but do take care."

Beneath the airship they all stare.
However will they get up there?

Rupert leaves his old kite with the Chinese Conjurer and the friends hurry off, with Rupert clutching the kite bag tightly. They get permission from Mrs Trunk, and then the chums set off for Rupert's house and repeat their story excitedly to Mrs Bear, who listens quietly. She thinks it sounds like a great adventure, but she is worried about the airship.

"I'm sure you will have lots of fun," she says as she waves them off, "but do take care!"

Rupert, Edward and Tigerlily make their way back to the Common, where the airship is waiting for them. The gigantic vehicle hovers high above, casting a huge black shadow on the ground. They can hear the whirr of the motors overhead.

"Goodness!" gulps Edward. "However are we going to get up there? Will it come down?"

"I don't think it will risk landing on the Common," ponders Rupert thoughtfully. "The wind is too strong."

RUPERT FLIES TO THE FESTIVAL

A door slides open with a swish.
Out comes a metal flying fish!

It picks them up one at a time.
Into the airship they all climb.

Young Rupert's last to take the ride.
Now they're all safely sat inside.

The motor starts and up they fly
So quickly through the Nutwood sky.

Then they hear a whooshing sound. A door slides open in the side of the airship and a shiny metal fish flashes out! It swoops down through the sky to land in front of them.

Sitting on the flying fish is a strange fellow who beckons first to Tigerlily. She goes to sit behind him on the flying fish and he flies up again into the sky. Rupert and Edward watch anxiously as the flying fish takes Tigerlily to the airship, turns around and comes back

down. Edward goes next, and then it's Rupert's turn.

When they're all safely aboard, the ship's engine cranks up speed, the whirring becomes a loud roar and the airship moves off. The friends look anxiously out over Nutwood Common.

"There's my house!" points Edward Trunk.

Then they leave the Common and, picking up speed, they fly past the Chinese Pagoda, leaving their familiar surroundings behind them.

RUPERT MEETS TWO VILLAINS

The airship soon comes to a stop
And drops them on a bare hilltop.

Then, as the airship flies away,
The chums set off without delay.

But suddenly they hear a shout
And two big ruffians jump out.

They snatch the bag and laugh with scorn.
"Don't open it!" the three chums warn.

The airship journeys above the clouds and soon the three friends are wondering where they will land. After a long journey, the airship descends through a blanket of cloud and they are greeted with a wonderful view of snow-capped mountains and deep river valleys.

Before long, the airship comes to rest on a bare hilltop. Tigerlily, Edward and Rupert clamber out. A rocky path leads down the hillside towards the entrance to the festival in the valley.

As the airship flies off, the three friends make their way down the hill. Suddenly, they hear a gruff shout.

"Halt where you are!" comes a voice. The friends all come to a stop, alarmed.

Two big ruffians jump out from behind the rocks and stand in their path.

"Hand over that bag!" growls the first ruffian.

"I c-c-can't," stammers Rupert. "It's not mine."

But the ruffian snatches it from Rupert anyway.

THE MAGIC KITE ESCAPES

The tallest scoundrel snarls, then gapes.
Too late! The magic kite escapes.

The Golden Carp attacks with glee.
The ruffians yelp, turn round and flee!

It chases them along the track.
They're both too frightened to look back.

But then the Golden Carp turns round
And lifts poor Rupert off the ground!

"Well, what have we here?" the ruffian snarls. "Is it something very precious?"

"I told you," says Rupert bravely, "it doesn't belong to me. Please give it back at once."

"Well, I might give you back the bag," sniggers the ruffian, "but I'm keeping whatever is inside." And with that, he looks inside.

"Don't!" cry the friends, but it's too late! The scoundrel opens the bag and releases the magic kite.

The pals gasp as the kite swoops up into the sky. It unfurls in the shape of a golden carp with a long, swirling tail. The robbers gape in surprise as the kite dives on them as though it were about to gobble them up. With a yelp they turn and run, and the golden carp chases them along the path.

The chums laugh as they watch the robbers flee empty-handed, but suddenly the golden kite turns on them and whooshes round and round!

31

RUPERT IS TANGLED IN THE KITE

It scoops the friends up with its tail
And through the clear blue sky they sail.

Above the festival they fly,
As they climb higher in the sky.

And then, at last, the kite heads down,
Towards a palace on the ground.

It seems the kite knows where to go.
It flies in through a small window.

The kite's tail wraps around the astonished friends, lifting them off the ground, and they sail through the air, high above the valley. Far below them they see brightly-coloured kites flapping in the breeze.

"That must be the kite festival down there!" shouts Tigerlily above the sound of the wind.

"However are we going to get down?" groans Edward, but there is no way for the friends to control the Golden Carp.

The three pals have no idea where they are going, but the Golden Carp seems to know! In the distance, a mighty palace appears before them and they begin to descend towards it.

"Do you think this is where the Emperor lives?" marvels Edward.

"I think I can see the entrance," says Rupert, but the Golden Carp suddenly swoops in through a small window and they find themselves in a very grand room.

RUPERT MEETS THE EMPEROR

The friends are dropped, and there they land
Before someone who's very grand.

"Hello! There is no need to fear.
The Conjurer knows I've brought you here."

"Now, Rupert, you will fly this kite.
The Golden Carp is quite a sight!"

The Emperor's son, the young prince John,
Says, "Will you all please come along?"

The kite gently releases the friends, dropping them in front of a large throne, upon which sits a very grand person. All around the room, guards stand to attention. Rupert, Edward and Tigerlily clamber to their feet.

"Greetings!" declares the tall figure. "I am the Emperor. Welcome, Tigerlily, and welcome also to your friends!"

The three friends bow their heads respectfully.

"I am delighted that you have brought the Golden Carp safely to my kite festival," continues the Emperor. "The Chinese Conjurer makes all my kites for me.

I particularly wish you, Rupert, to fly the Golden Carp this year."

The chums tell the Emperor all about the two ruffians who tried to steal it and how they escaped.

"There is someone I'd like you to meet," says the Emperor. "This is my son, Prince John."

RUPERT FLIES THE GOLDEN CARP

He takes them to a special hall.
Inside, great kites adorn each wall.

The friends choose kites to take away
That they'll fly later on that day.

A gentle breeze then blows just right
For everyone to fly their kites.

A hundred kites, all flying high.
They look fantastic in the sky!

Rupert, Edward and Tigerlily follow the prince through a maze of rooms to a huge hall. The friends gasp when they step inside. Kites of every shape and colour hang from the walls.

"As our most honoured guests," smiles Prince John, "the Emperor requests that you each select a kite to fly at our festival." The chums can't believe their luck!

Edward spots a colourful box kite. "I've always wanted to fly one of those," he declares delightedly.

Tigerlily chooses one that is red and yellow with a long tail. Prince John selects his own favourite and then leads his new friends out of the palace.

Before long they come to the festival, and soon the friends' kites are flying in the strong breeze. The sky is filled with colourful shapes all dipping and diving.

The friends are having tremendous fun. The crowd of onlookers are impressed by their aerobatic tricks and clap enthusiastically.

But Rupert's kite flies at the crowd!
"Watch out there!" Rupert shouts aloud.

The kite's found something, Rupert's sure.
It's those two ruffians from before!

The scoundrels have been stealing things –
Like wallets, purses, keys and rings.

The emperor's guard thanks Rupert Bear
For capturing the crooked pair.

Rupert has been struggling to hold on to his kite in the breeze when suddenly he feels the string go slack. Poor Rupert cannot control the kite and he watches aghast as the Golden Carp dives into the crowd.

"Watch out, there!" Rupert cries, but then he spots the two robbers from earlier and realises the Golden Carp is going to chase after them again! Rupert alerts the security guards as the amazing kite wraps itself around the villains.

The guards make the robbers turn out their pockets. They produce all kinds of valuable things that don't belong to them – wallets, purses, keys and rings. The wicked pair have been lurking in the crowd stealing from people's pockets while they watched the kite-flying!

The two scoundrels are brought before the Emperor. He is delighted that they have been caught red-handed and sends them to jail.

But soon it's time to say goodbye.
The airship is prepared to fly.

Still, after their exciting break,
The fearless friends are wide awake!

The airship sails toward the sun.
The friends agree they've had great fun.

Then Rupert runs home – he can't wait
To meet his mother at the gate.

As a reward, he invites the three friends to attend the festival banquet. There are sandwiches and cakes and jellies of every description, and everyone has a wonderful time. Finally, the Emperor and Prince John come to say farewell. The airship is ready to take them home.

Once more, the friends climb aboard the airship. Although it has been a very long and tiring day, they are far too excited to go to sleep.

As they draw near to Nutwood the wind drops, and the airship touches down gently on Nutwood Common. The tired friends clamber out and watch as the airship flies off towards the setting sun, until it is just a tiny speck on the horizon.

"Well, that was terrific fun," remarks Edwards

"I hope we can go again next year," sighs Tigerlily.

Mrs Bear is waiting by the gate to meet Rupert when he gets home.

RUPERT'S KITE IS MENDED

As Rupert turns to go inside,
Mrs Bear sees something glide.

And Rupert feels a gentle smack –
There's something tapping on his back.

"My kite is mended!" Rupert cries,
As magically it spins and dives.

Then Rupert looks back up the track,
And spies his friends there, waving back!

Rupert tells his mum about the airship ride, the two robbers and, most of all, the marvellous kite-flying festival. As he turns to go into the cottage, Mrs Bear notices something gliding up the garden path.

"What you need is your own magic kite," she says, wisely.

Then Rupert feels a gentle tap on his back. He turns around expecting to see his mum, but he gets a big surprise – it's his old kite!

"It's been mended!" cries Rupert, delightedly. "And the Conjurer has worked some magic on it too!" Rupert can't believe his luck.

He looks back and, standing on the brow of the hill, silhouetted against the sunset, the Chinese Conjurer and Tigerlily are waving to him.

Rupert waves back happily.

"Thank you," he whispers into the gentle evening breeze.

GOLDEN CARP KITE ORIGAMI

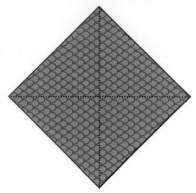

With the coloured side up, fold in half on both diagonals, then unfold.

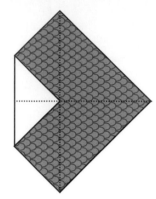

Fold one corner into the centre point, then unfold.

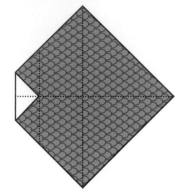

Fold the same corner to meet the crease you just made.

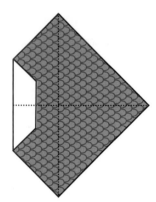

Refold on the original crease line.

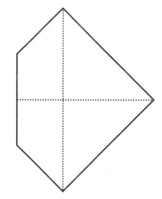

Flip so the white side is up.

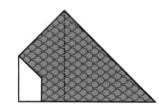

Bring up the bottom corner to meet the top corner.

Fold the top corner down to meet the bottom edge.

Make two small folds on each end, as shown above. Glue them if necessary.

Flip over, glue on an eye and decorate it. Now glue it on a string or lolly stick!

SPOT THE DIFFERENCE

The pictures above look the same, but there are ten small differences in picture 2. Look closely! Can you spot them all?

RUPERT'S WORD SEARCH

P	I	C	L	I	V	E	B	W	H	A	P	K
L	R	N	X	A	R	N	W	G	M	O	R	J
F	C	S	T	D	L	C	U	B	V	Z	U	A
Y	A	R	Q	N	E	G	S	H	E	E	P	C
F	X	L	A	B	E	P	Y	M	O	N	E	W
E	T	D	W	G	A	L	H	K	B	S	R	V
I	K	M	N	I	G	U	V	Q	J	P	T	G
H	J	A	U	S	L	Y	O	M	U	A	C	M
T	E	U	O	M	E	W	S	B	M	E	R	O
Q	I	S	A	R	A	F	G	T	P	K	E	N
G	R	O	W	L	E	R	L	X	E	W	G	F
P	N	T	Y	N	D	J	Q	J	R	E	Z	I
S	H	E	L	I	C	R	A	F	T	C	P	J

Uncle Clive's sheep are lost in this word grid, along with other characters and objects from the next story. Can you find them all? Words can be read up, down, sideways and diagonally.

ALGY, BEN, CLIVE, EAGLE, CRAGGY STEEP, GROWLER, HELICRAFT, JUMPER, MUM, RUPERT, SHEEP, THIEF

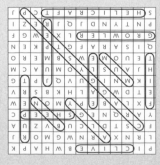

RUPERT
and the
Lost Sheep

RUPERT WANTS TO VISIT HIS UNCLE

One night, when Mum is busy knitting,
Rupert sits down where she's sitting.

The wool is from his uncle's sheep.
His farm is close to Craggy Steep.

Says Rupert Bear, "I'd like to go
To visit Uncle Clive, you know."

Then Rupert runs to ask his chum
Young Algy Pug, if he can come.

It's holiday time, and one evening Rupert watches his mum busily knitting a jumper.

"Where does your wool come from?" asks Rupert.

"This wool comes from your Uncle Clive's sheep," replies Mrs Bear. "He has a farm in a place called Craggy Steep."

"Why have we never been there?" asks Rupert.

"It's a long way away," sighs Mrs Bear. Rupert goes to fetch his atlas and looks it up on the map.

"I'd like to visit Uncle Clive's farm. Please may I go to stay with him?" asks Rupert hopefully.

"I'll phone him to ask," says Mrs Bear.

She is smiling when she comes back. "Uncle Clive says he will be delighted to see you," she reports, "and he thinks you should bring a friend."

"Hurray!" grins Rupert. "I'll go and ask Algy Pug if he can come."

Algy is very pleased to be asked.

RUPERT SETS OFF FOR CRAGGY STEEP

Poor Mrs Bear tries not to fuss
As they are waiting for the bus.

And now the two friends pay their fare,
Sit down and wave to Mrs Bear.

The country road begins to wind
And Nutwood is soon left behind.

"I say! What's that?" young Algy cries.
"There's something strange up in the skies."

Early the next morning, Mrs Bear and Rupert meet Algy at the bus stop. Uncle Clive has warned them that the weather is colder in the mountains, so the two friends are wearing stout walking boots and waterproof coats.

At last they see the bus making its way towards them. The friends climb on board and pay their fares. As the bus pulls off, they turn and wave goodbye.

Then the chums settle down for the long journey.

After some time, the road begins to wind higher and the friends watch out of the window as the view changes from rolling hills to steep-sided mountains.

"I say," gasps Algy Pug. "What's that?" He points at a strange-looking craft buzzing in the sky.

"Gosh!" exclaims Rupert. "I've never seen anything like it before. I wonder what it can be?" But the weird flying machine soon disappears from view behind a lofty mountain peak.

RUPERT RIDES IN A HORSE AND TRAP

The bus stops and the chums get out
But there is no one else about.

Then comes along a horse and trap.
It's driven by a cheerful chap.

The driver stops and, with a grin,
He greets the boys and lifts them in.

"Your uncle sent me from the farm
To make sure you come to no harm."

"Next stop – Craggy Steep," calls the driver from the front of the bus.

"That's us!" cries Rupert excitedly.

The friends jump down from the bus. They wave as the bus slowly pulls off and makes its way up the winding pass. There is no one waiting at the bus stop.

"I hope your Uncle Clive hasn't forgotten we're coming," says Algy Pug anxiously. Then they hear the clip-clop of a horse making its way towards them.

The driver stops and hops down from his trap.

"You must be Rupert and Algy," he grins. "Your uncle sent me to pick you up."

"Why, he's not ill is he?" asks Rupert alarmed.

"No, don't worry," says the driver. "He had to sort out some trouble with his sheep."

The driver helps the two friends into the back of the trap. "Hold on tight!" he calls as the cart bumps along the rocky mountain road.

RUPERT HEARS ABOUT THE LOST SHEEP

And soon enough, there's Uncle Clive.
"I hope you boys enjoyed the drive!"

The chums sit down, their faces beam
To see a tea of scones and cream.

Says Uncle Clive, "My sheep are lost.
They must be found, at any cost."

The two chums settle down to sleep
And dream of finding his lost sheep.

At last they arrive at the farm and Uncle Clive is waiting to greet them. "I hope you've had a good journey," he says, shaking Rupert by the hand.

Uncle Clive shows them around the farmyard where Ben the sheepdog is barking noisily. He is excited to have two new pals to play with.

Inside, the farmhouse is warm and cosy, and the kitchen table is laid out all ready for tea. There are plates of scones, homemade jam and a jug of cream.

That evening, Rupert, Algy and Uncle Clive sit around the fireside, sipping mugs of hot cocoa. Rupert suddenly remembers what the driver said earlier that day. "Did you sort out the trouble with your sheep, Uncle Clive?" he asks.

"I'm afraid some of my sheep have gone missing," sighs Uncle Clive. "Perhaps you two could help me look for them tomorrow?"

"We'd like that," smiles Rupert sleepily.

RUPERT SEES A STRANGER

With Ben the sheepdog off they go
To search the hillside, high and low.

Before too long, the climb gets steep,
But still they haven't seen one sheep.

Then Rupert spots, as he looks back,
A stranger standing on the track.

And when they climb round Craggy Steep,
They find the missing flock of sheep!

The next morning, they are all up early. Ben the sheepdog leads the way out of the farmyard towards the mountain track. He runs ahead, barking excitedly for the friends to follow.

"Keep a steady pace!" warns Uncle Clive. "We've a long, hard climb ahead of us."

The track grows narrower and fainter until it peters out altogether. Now they have to find their own way up the mountainside.

They clamber up the steep, rocky slope and stop to rest at the top. They can see Uncle Clive's farmhouse far below. Gazing around, Rupert sees someone standing on the mountain track, but he is too far away to make out clearly.

They make their way to the far side of the mountain, when Ben starts barking excitedly. He's found the missing sheep! The grazing flock look up, unperturbed to see the friends scrambling down toward them.

RUPERT HERDS THE SHEEP

Then Uncle Clive says, "Now you two,
We'll round them up – here's what to do."

And so the friends begin to shout,
While Ben the sheepdog runs about.

The chums help herd the sheep and then
They guide the flock into the pen.

But Uncle Clive looks with a frown.
He counts the sheep, but he's five down.

Uncle Clive is delighted! "Now we can round them up and herd them back down to the pen," he says.

Uncle Clive tells the two friends where to stand and what to do. Uncle Clive stands quietly at a distance and makes a complicated series of whistles. At each sound, Ben the sheepdog moves closer to the sheep or darts around the back of the flock to keep them moving together. The pals stand with their arms held wide in case a stray sheep wanders away from the flock.

Working together, they drive the flock back over the brow of the hill to lower pasture. Rupert and Algy run ahead to open the gate of the sheep pen and they stand either side to help guide the sheep back in.

At last, the flock are in the pen and the gate is closed. The friends stand on the fence while Uncle Clive counts up his sheep. But he's looking worried.

"Hmm," he ponders. "I've counted them three times. There are definitely five sheep still missing."

They leave the sheep safe in the pen
And all set off to look again.

Then Uncle Clive trips in the dirt.
He can't get up – his ankle's hurt.

"I don't think I can walk, I fear,
So you will have to leave me here."

"You go for help," says Rupert Bear,
"While I keep searching over there."

They leave the sheep in the pen and set off to search again for the missing ones. Uncle Clive leads the way as they climb higher and higher, until they are walking over bare rock and gravel. It's very steep and slippery underfoot. Suddenly, the two chums hear a cry!

They turn and are dismayed to see Uncle Clive at the bottom of the slope. He has slipped on the loose scree and taken a tumble. Rupert and Algy make their way gingerly back down.

"Hold on, Uncle Clive," calls Rupert, anxiously. "We're coming down to help."

Uncle Clive has hurt his ankle. "I don't think I can walk," he says glumly. "You will have to leave me here and go to get help."

The two friends make sure Uncle Clive is comfortable before scrambling back up the slope.

"You go for help, Algy," says Rupert, "and I'll carry on searching for the missing sheep."

Now high up, Rupert sees once more
The strange man that he saw before.

The stranger drives the sheep away
Rupert follows without delay.

But Rupert's spotted by the man,
Who captures him and makes a plan.

He takes the sheep and Rupert higher.
Poor Rupert soon begins to tire.

Ben the sheepdog trots alongside Rupert. They come across a mountain track, and Rupert spots some fresh sheep droppings.

"I think the sheep must be close by," he smiles at Ben. As he looks up, Rupert spies the stranger he saw earlier making his way along the track. The man is driving some sheep ahead of him, so the brave little bear decides to follow.

Rupert and Ben follow at a distance as the man drives the small flock higher and higher into the mountains, then Rupert loses sight of him as he crosses a rocky ridge. The sheep reappear, but the stranger is not with them.

"Gotcha!" growls a voice from behind. The sheep-stealer jumps out and grabs Rupert before he has time to run away.

"Thought you'd caught me, did you?" the man accuses. "Well, now I've caught you!"

BEN HELPS RUPERT TO ESCAPE

They cross a bridge that's very high.
The frightened bear can't help but sigh.

Then Rupert's bound, his clothes get torn.
Left all alone, he feels forlorn.

Brave Ben comes running up the slope.
He's followed them. He chews the rope!

Now straight away they free the sheep
And herd them back to Craggy Steep.

The villain takes him further and further away from Craggy Steep. After a while, Rupert realises that Ben the sheepdog is nowhere to be seen.

"Oh no," thinks Rupert. "How will I ever find my way back without Ben?" Eventually they arrive at a rocky shelter where the villain puts the sheep in a pen. Then he turns to Rupert holding a thick rope. Rupert puts up a brave fight as the robber ties him up, and his jumper gets torn in the struggle.

The robber disappears inside the shelter, leaving Rupert tied up against a rock. Poor Rupert looks around for something to cut the rope, but there's nothing that can help him. Just then, he hears panting behind him and a wet nose pushes at his sleeve.

The brave sheepdog has followed him and chews through the rope! Rupert creeps quietly towards the sheep pen and lifts open the gate. Ben urges the sheep out of the pen and they make their way back home.

They hurry through the rough terrain,
But then the man spots them again!

He chases them along the track.
Poor Rupert doesn't dare look back.

Around the bend, no time to rest,
They see an eagle on its nest.

The eagle squawks a mighty call,
The man jumps back and starts to fall.

It isn't long before the robber realises that Rupert has escaped with the sheep. He comes running after them. "Come back!" he shouts angrily.

The robber chases after Rupert and Ben along the narrow mountain track. They run as fast as they can, but the sheep slow them down. Rupert doesn't dare look back. He can hear the sheep-stealer's footsteps getting closer and closer. As they round a tight bend, Rupert sees a giant eagle sitting on its nest.

"What's the great hurry?" the eagle asks.

"We're escaping from a villain who tried to steal my uncle's sheep," pants Rupert. "I'm very sorry, I don't have time to stop!"

"I think I might be able to help you," says the eagle thoughtfully. Rupert hurries on, but as the robber rounds the bend he hears a loud SQUAWK! Rupert looks back to see the surprised villain lose his balance and tumble over the edge!

RUPERT SEES THE HELICRAFT

Then Rupert turns and sees him drop,
Though he's afraid, he has to stop.

But then he sees the eagle swoop
And catch the man in one neat scoop.

"Thank you!" shouts Rupert with a grin.
"Old PC Growler can deal with him!"

Just then, they see high in the sky
The helicraft come flying by.

"Oh no!" Rupert cries in dismay, stopping in his tracks as he sees the sheep-stealer fall. He starts to run back but there is nothing he can do to save him.

But the giant eagle spreads its mighty wings and swoops down beneath the falling villain. Its massive claws grab the man out of the air and carry him back up into the sky.

"Thanks!" Rupert calls with a grin. "Please take him to PC Growler. He'll know what to do with a thief!"

Rupert and Ben wind their way back along the valley until they finally reach Uncle Clive. Rupert tells him about the sheep-stealer and the eagle.

"Well, I'm very relieved to see you all back safely," grimaces Uncle Clive. His ankle is still very painful. Then Rupert hears the sound of an engine close by. It's coming from a small helicraft.

"That's the strange machine we saw yesterday," marvels Rupert. "Maybe it has come to rescue us!"

Rupert and the Lost Sheep

RUPERT HELPS UNCLE CLIVE

And Algy Pug comes into view,
The old Professor's with him too!

The helicraft sets down close by.
They've come to rescue Uncle Clive.

They help poor Uncle Clive toward
The helicraft and climb aboard.

Then everybody says goodbye,
And off to hospital they fly.

Rupert stands up and waves madly at the helicraft, but he needn't have worried. It has already spotted them. As it flies in closer, he can see Algy Pug waving back and the Professor at the controls. They have come to rescue Uncle Clive.

In no time at all, they have landed safely. Algy jumps out, followed by the Professor. The Professor examines Uncle Clive's ankle and shakes his head. "It's serious," he remarks gravely, "but, don't worry, you'll soon be on the mend."

Uncle Clive winces as he tries to get up. His ankle is very painful to walk on. He leans on the Professor's shoulder and limps to the helicraft. Then the Professor climbs back behind the controls and starts the engine.

"Don't worry about the sheep, Uncle Clive," calls Rupert. "We'll make sure they get back to the farm safely." Rupert and Algy wave farewell as the helicraft carries Uncle Clive off to the hospital.

RUPERT AND ALGY HERD THE SHEEP

The chums still have a job to do,
And Ben the dog can help them too.

They herd the flock down to the farm,
Where sheep can graze away from harm.

Poor Uncle Clive leans on his crutch.
"Now, don't forget to keep in touch!"

What an exciting holiday!
"I'll see you soon," the two friends say.

"Come on, Ben," says Rupert, "we still have a job to do." And with the faithful dog's help, the two chums start rounding up the sheep.

"What luck!" Algy explains. "The helicraft spotted me coming down the mountain and thought I was lost, so the Professor landed next to me. He was trying out his new invention, you see."

Soon the chums are back at the farm, and the lost sheep join the rest of their flock in the pen.

Later that evening the Professor brings Uncle Clive back from hospital. Poor Uncle Clive's foot is encased in plaster and he hobbles about with the help of a crutch. "My ankle is broken, I'm afraid," he sighs. "I don't know what I would have done if it hadn't been for you two."

The next morning, Uncle Clive and Ben accompany the two pals to the bus stop. "Don't forget to keep in touch!" he calls as he waves them goodbye.

RUPERT HAS A SURPRISE

On his way home, young Rupert sees
The wicked thief and the police.

The PC says, "Now don't you fear.
I'll take him far away from here."

Now Rupert's glad to see his mum.
"My jumper's torn – it's come undone."

"Come on," says Mum, "Don't feel so blue.
I've made a new one, just for you!"

Later, as Rupert crosses Nutwood Common on his way home, he sees the sheep-stealer being escorted by PC Growler.

"Why, it's that dratted bear!" growls the villain as they approach.

"That's enough of that!" says PC Growler sternly. He turns to Rupert. "I hope your Uncle Clive is feeling better," he says, kindly. "And don't worry about this scoundrel – he won't be bothering anyone for a while!"

Rupert hurries home, and tells his mother the whole story. "I've ruined my best jumper," he says glumly. Mrs Bear carefully examines the tear in his sleeve.

"I'm sure I can darn this," she smiles. "But until it's mended, it's just as well I've finished knitting this one!" Mrs Bear holds up a brand new jumper.

"A new jumper for me!" exclaims Rupert delightedly. "Thank you! And it's made from Uncle Clive's wool, so it will remind me of my adventure!"

THE LOST SHEEP MAZE

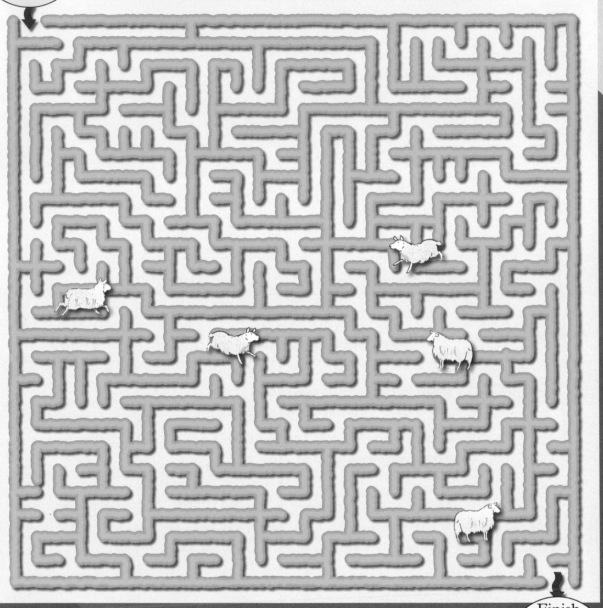

Start

Finish

Rupert is searching for Uncle Clive's five lost sheep. Can you guide him from Craggy Steep to the farm, passing all five sheep along the way?

Answer:

RUPERT
and the
Cut

RUPERT GOES TO PICK BLACKBERRIES

When Rupert sees the apple tree,
He asks, "Can we have pie for tea?"

"I'll need some blackberries," says Mum.
"Would you go out and fetch me some?"

Bill Badger wants to help him too.
"Can I come blackberrying with you?"

And soon they spot a bush nearby.
"No blackberries here," the two chums sigh.

One sunny day, Rupert is in the garden helping Mrs Bear gather apples from the tree.

"May I eat one?" he asks his mum.

"These are not eating apples," explains Mrs Bear, "they're cooking apples."

"What would happen if I ate one?" asks Rupert.

"It would give you a very sore tummy," Mrs Bear replies. "But they're delicious cooked in a pie."

"Can we have a pie for tea?" Rupert asks excitedly.

"Yes," laughs Mrs Bear. "But it would taste even nicer with some blackberries in it. Will you collect some from the Common for me, please?"

Then Bill Badger arrives. "What are you up to?"

"I'm collecting blackberries for a pie," says Rupert.

"Can I come too?" asks Bill.

Rupert is delighted, so he and Bill set off for the Common. Before long they spot a big bramble bush, but there are no blackberries on it.

RUPERT MEETS FREDDY AND FERDY

Then Freddy Fox comes into view.
(His brother Ferdy is there too.)

The foxes tell the hapless pair,
"You'll find some blackberries over there!"

So off they go to look again,
But still their searching is in vain.

"Well, all the fruit seems to have gone,"
Says Rupert. "Let's look further on."

The chums walk further and further, but they can't find any blackberries on the bushes. Then they spot Freddy and Ferdy Fox.

"Do you think they know where to find some blackberries?" Bill wonders.

"Let's ask," says Rupert. "Hello, Freddy! Have you seen any blackberries?"

"Heaps!" boasts Freddy Fox. "I know where to find all the best blackberry bushes in Nutwood."

"Where should we look?" asks Rupert.

"Over that way," Freddy sniggers, pointing to some large brambles, and then he turns and runs off in the opposite direction!

Rupert and Bill search high and low, but they still can't find a single blackberry! They are very puzzled.

"We're not having much luck!" grumbles Bill.

"It doesn't look as though we'll be having pie for tea after all," sighs Rupert.

RUPERT IS STARTLED BY AN IMP

"Look! Here's a likely bush," says Bill.
They see a young girl on the hill.

They call out to the girl, "I say!"
But she turns tail and runs away.

Then Rupert gives a startled shout,
As from the bush, an imp jumps out.

"Stop stealing!" he shouts angrily.
"These blackberries are just for me!"

But the friends are not ready to give up yet!
"There's a likely patch," exclaims Bill, cheering up.
"There are bound to be some blackberries there."

The chums run over to the bush and, as they search, they overhear voices in the distance. There are two figures standing on the hill. It looks like Freddy Fox again, and he's talking to a small girl in a pink dress.

Then, Rupert spots a bush loaded with blackberries!
"Look!" he shouts to Bill. "There are more than

enough blackberries there to make a pie."

They start to pick the berries, but suddenly an angry imp jumps out from the bush. "Stop stealing our berries!" he shrieks. "These are *our* berries."

"We're very sorry," gulps Rupert. "We had no idea anyone lived here."

"Shoo!" cries the imp. "Go find your own berries!"

The disappointed friends take their basket and walk down towards the canal.

RUPERT MEETS BILL THE BARGEE

Bill Badger gives a mournful sigh,
Then something white attracts his eye.

What was that little puff of smoke?
It's Bargee Bill on the Sally Oak!

"I know a blackberry bush," says Bill.
"It's past the Cut on Blackberry Hill.

"I'll take you there – no extra charge!"
And so the chums jump on the barge.

The chums are beginning to think they will never collect any blackberries. Then they spot a puff of smoke in the distance and a narrowboat comes chugging down the canal.

"I think I recognise that barge," exclaims Rupert. "Isn't it the *Sally Oak*?"

"By golly, you're right Rupert," says Bill, as it approaches. The two friends wait on the towpath until the barge comes alongside.

"Hello, lads," Bill the bargee greets them. "What are you doing up here?"

"We're blackberrying," replies Rupert. "The only trouble is, we can't find any! Do you know where else we can look?"

"You could try past the Cut on Blackberry Hill," he suggests. "I'm going that way if you want a ride."

"Rather!" say the two pals.

"No charge," laughs Bill as they jump on board.

RUPERT OPENS THE LOCK GATES

So soon the barge chugs to a stop.
They've reached the lock, and off they hop.

The two friends open up the gates,
While Bill the bargee sits and waits.

The Sally Oak sinks slowly down,
Then something makes young Rupert frown.

Who's throwing blackberries in the lock?
It's Freddy Fox and Ferdy Fox!

The *Sally Oak* putters along the canal until they see a sign on the towpath warning them to slow down. Bargee Bill slows the engine and the barge chugs to a halt. They've reached the lock. The pals jump off the barge and push the two lock gates open.

Bargee Bill eases the barge inside the lock and throws a rope up to the lads. They quickly tie it to a bollard and watch, fascinated, as the bottom sluice gates open and the water roars out of the lock.

The water falls quickly, taking the barge down to the level of the next part of the canal. Then, above the noise of the water, they hear Bargee Bill give a shout and they see two figures throwing blackberries into the lock. It's Freddy and Ferdy Fox up to mischief again! Where did they find all those blackberries? The two naughty foxes run away when Bargee Bill shakes his fist. Rupert and Bill still have work to do. They open the next set of lock gates and release the rope.

RUPERT FINDS A LOST GIRL

Now here's that girl they've seen around.
She's sitting crying on the ground.

"When I was picking fruit today,
Two foxes sent me the wrong way.

"And now I'm lost," the small girl cries.
"Those naughty foxes told me lies!"

"You can't go this way on your own."
Says Bargee Bill, "We'll take you home."

Rupert and Bill hop back on to the *Sally Oak* and sit on the roof. Up ahead, they see a little girl in a pink dress standing by the tunnel.

"I say," exclaims Rupert. "That's the same girl we saw earlier, and she's crying."

"I wonder why she's upset?" says Bill Badger. "We'd better find out."

The *Sally Oak* stops just before the Cut and Rupert jumps off to see if he can help.

"I was looking for blackberries near the Common," the girls sobs, "when I met a fox."

"That was Freddy," Rupert tells her.

"He told me where I could find some more berries," continues the girl, "but that naughty fox told me lies. He sent me the wrong way and now I'm lost."

"Well, you can't go through the tunnel on your own," says Bargee Bill. "Hop on board and we'll take you home."

RUPERT MEETS THE LEGGER ELVES

Just then, the legger elves appear.
"We'll take you through the Cut, don't fear!"

The tunnel's long and dark inside.
The little chaps work hard, with pride!

The legger elves walk on the wall
And nudge the barge through at a crawl.

While down below, all warm and snug,
The friends drink cocoa from a mug.

Just then, a window opens in the side of the tunnel and a little face appears. It's one of the legger elves.

"We'll take your barge through the Cut, don't fear."

Bargee Bill turns off the engine so the smoke doesn't fill the air. The elves hurry to either side of the barge, leaning their backs against the roof and bracing their legs against the side of the tunnel. They chant a barge song with a steady beat as they walk along the walls, dragging the barge through the long, dark passage.

Meanwhile, down in the cosy, snug cabin, Bill Badger chats with their new friend while they enjoy cocoa and biscuits. She tells him that she lives in a bakery in the next town. Her father is the baker.

"I was out collecting some blackberries to make a pie," she explains.

"So were we!" laughs Bill. Suddenly, they see Rupert's head peering in at them upside down through the window, making them both laugh out loud!

RUPERT PICKS SOME BLACKBERRIES

And then, ahead, they see some light.
At last the tunnel's end's in sight!

Beyond the Cut and past some trees,
They stop to pick their blackberries.

Then, on an aqueduct they go,
And gaze down at the town below.

The girl says, "Look there, I can see
My home – it's at that bakery."

At last, they see daylight at the far end of the tunnel, and before long the *Sally Oak* emerges into the sunlight. The friends thank the legger elves for their hard work before the elves disappear back inside the Cut to await the next barge.

Then Bargee Bill shows the chums the most glorious blackberry bush crammed with berries. They can't believe their luck! Bargee Bill waits while the pals pick as many blackberries as they can carry.

The air is filled with the sweet smell of ripe berries and everyone is feeling very happy when they hop back onto the barge. The *Sally Oak* chugs along steadily over an aqueduct that carries them high above the town. It's very strange sailing past the rooftops!

Suddenly, the little girl spots her home. "There's the bakery," she cries delightedly. "That's where I live."

The pals leave a big bowl of blackberries in the cabin to thank Bargee Bill for the ride.

RUPERT TAKES THE GIRL HOME

"Thanks, Bill," they shout as they jump down.
He waves as they set off through town.

At last, they're at the bakery.
They get there just in time for tea!

They tell their story as they eat.
The baker's cooked a super treat.

"Perhaps your mum would like to try
My blackberry and apple pie?"

Bargee Bill stops the *Sally Oak* and the chums all jump out.

"Thanks, Bill," they call, waving goodbye, and off they hurry through the town to the bakery.

"Would you like to stay for tea?" asks the little girl. There's a splendid spread of cakes, sandwiches, pie and custard, and as they eat, the little girl tells her mum and dad how she got lost and how Rupert and Bill rescued her and brought her safely home.

Just then, the little girl's father appears from the kitchen. He has brought them a special thank-you gift for bringing his daughter back safely – a freshly-baked blackberry and apple pie!

After tea, Rupert and Bill make their way back to Nutwood. It's a long walk home. When they get to Bill's house, they share out the blackberries.

"What a great day," beams Bill Badger. "I never thought blackberrying would be so much fun!"

Rupert and the Cut

RUPERT SEES THE FOX BROTHERS

As Rupert heads back home from town,
He sees the foxes lying down.

"Oh! We ate too much fruit," they moan,
"And now our tummies ache!" they groan.

Rupert thinks it serves them right.
And then his house comes into sight.

He's home at last. Mum gasps, "Oh my!
A blackberry and apple pie!"

Rupert takes a short cut across the Common on his way home. He hears a moan, and comes across Freddy and Ferdy Fox lying on the ground. Their whiskers and paws are stained purple. Rupert thinks he can guess what they've been up to.

"Hello, you two," says Rupert. "What's wrong?"

"We ate too many blackberries," groan the pair. "Now we have the most frightful tummy ache."

Rupert shakes his head as he walks on. He can't help thinking they deserve it for being so greedy.

Finally, his home comes into view and Rupert hurries in. "Home at last," he puffs.

"You've been out a long time," remarks Mrs Bear.

Rupert tells his mum the whole story. "I did find some blackberries in the end," he says, showing her his basket. "But look what else I have!" He presents his Mum with his surprise, and Mrs Bear is delighted.

"Well!" she gasps. "A blackberry and apple pie!"

RUPERT'S MEMORY TEST

1. What is Sailor Sam looking at?

2. Name the barge Rupert is riding in.

3. Who is holding Rupert by the collar?

4. What has Rupert seen in the sky?

5. What kind of pie is Rupert holding?

6. Rupert is drinking tea and eating what?

7. What is wrapped around the friends?

8. What is Sailor Sam driving?

9. What is in the bag?

10. What does the wand do to the trees?

11. What is Rupert doing?

12. What is the name of the sheepdog?

Try this memory test only when you have read the whole book. Each of the pictures above is taken from one of the stories you have read in this book. Study them carefully, then see if you can answer the questions.

Answer: 1. magic wand 2. *Sally Oak* 3. the sheep-stealer 4. an airship 5. blackberry and apple pie 6. scones 7. the Golden Carp kite's tail 8. amphibious car 9. a magic kite 10. it makes them re-grow 11. opening a lock gate 12. Ben.